*With all beings
and all things
we shall be
as relatives.*
—Sioux Indian

For Barry Jackson
who gave us
a place to live.

The Sunshine Family and the Pony

by Sharron Loree

THE SEABURY PRESS
New York

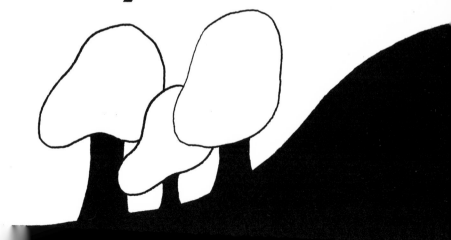

Once upon a time,
a lot of friends
wanted to move
out of the city
and live in the country.

After we got to our new home,
we had a meeting on the porch.

Betty said: "We used to be just friends,
but now we are a family."

Everyone agreed.
But who would clean the house
and cook the food?
Who would plant the garden?

We decided that everyone
would clean the house
and cook the food.
Those who wanted to
could plant the garden.

All the children decided
to sleep in the same room.

One day, our nearest neighbor called.
She said: "I have a good pony,
but no one rides her here.
Would your family like to have her?"

Judy said: "The children could ride her."
Julian said: "I would like that."
Mel said: "What do we need a pony for? We're farmers."
Gary said: "Let's eat!"

We didn't all agree, but because some of us
wanted the pony, we brought her home.

First
Laura
rode
the
pony

then
Julian

then
Pablo

then
Megan

then
Angus

then
Justin.

The pony didn't like being ridden very much.

Perhaps she needed to get used to us.

We fed her some grain and tied her to a tree.
It turned dark and we went to sleep.

In the morning we looked out the window
to see the pony.

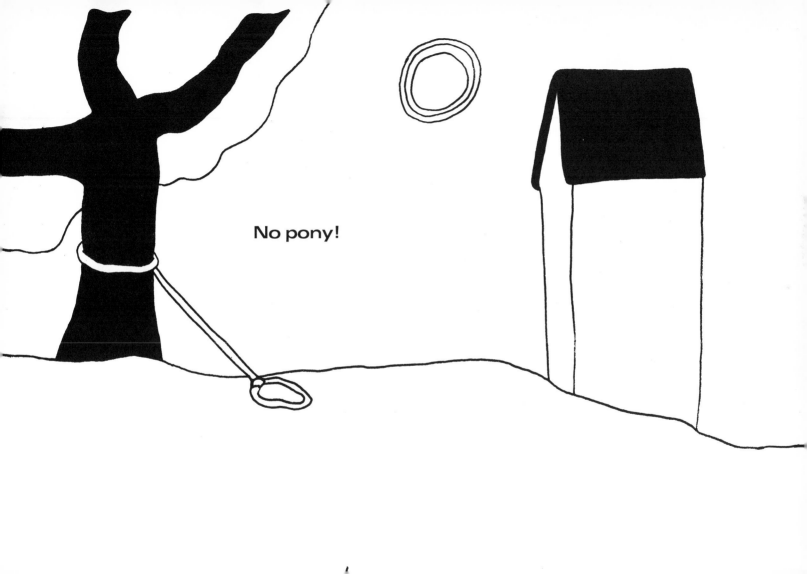

No pony!

"Wake up, Joel! Wake up, Buffy!"

"Wake up, Judy!"
Everyone got up
to look for the pony.

We looked in the garden

behind the house

and in the barn.

Megan and Buffy looked for hoofprints.

Justin and Julian
looked up and down.

Pablo, Angus, and Laura looked across fields.

Betty almost got lost in the woods when she was looking.

For three days it rained,
and we thought of our pony out in the rain.
Was she all right?
We left the barn door open for her.

The next three days were warm,
and we thought of our lost pony, far away.
Even Mel missed the pony.
He put grain on the road for her.

On the seventh day, a neighbor who
lived three miles away called.
"My little boy found a pony," she said.
"I think it is yours."

We hoped it would be our pony.

It was! We were so glad to see her.

We told the little boy to come over anytime and visit,
and we took the pony home.

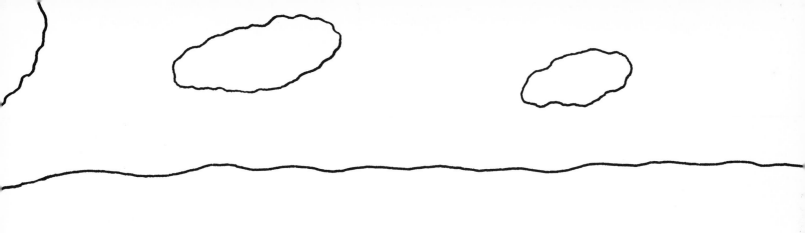

Every morning we gave the pony grain and water
and tied her very carefully to a tree.

We didn't ride her because
she still didn't want us to.

At night we put her in the barn.
She just didn't look happy. She didn't like
being tied to a tree or kept in the barn.

"Maybe she needs to be free," Justin said.

So the next day we built a fence around our garden.
Now the pony couldn't eat the vegetables.

Then we let her go.

She didn't go far. She walked around the garden
and ran across the field.

Then she came back.
The warm sun was shining down on us,
and we were all happy.

We felt like a Sunshine Family.